W9-ANJ-415

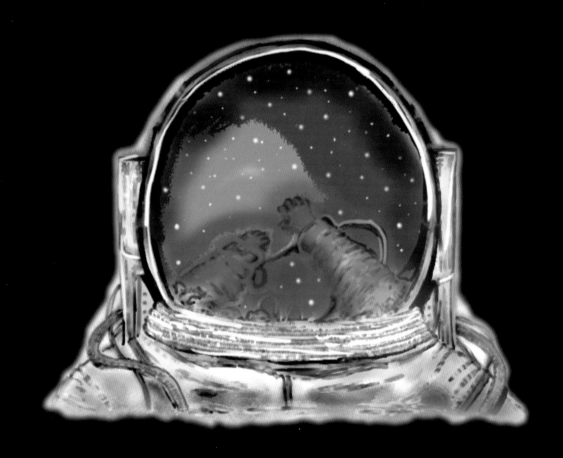

for my grandparents

for my nieces

BEYOND THINKING: for humanity

www.mascotbooks.com

BEYOND THE STARS

For more information, please contact:
Mascot Books
620 Herndon Parkway, Suite 320
Herndon, VA 20170
info@mascotbooks.com

Library of Congress Control Number: 2018914831

CPSIA Code: PRT0619A
ISBN-13: 978-1-68401-911-3

Printed in the United States

PROLOGUE

However many cultures there are in the world,

every culture counts.

However many religions there are in the world,

every religion counts.

However many humans there are in the world,

every human counts.

All is love, everywhere.

Come with me through the wormholes.

Listen to the teachings, listen to the values.

Come with me through the wormholes.

See humans,

see beauty,

see color,

see light.

Think beyond the stars...

A mother plays in the snow with
her daughter and tells her that how she
acts when no one is looking is what will
matter the most in life, as this will show her
morals and bring her closer to her inner truth.

"Mom, are morals beautiful?" she asks.

"Yes, the beauty of values goes beyond
the stars," she replies.

BEYOND THINKING: Moral values give meaning to life.

A brother brushes his sister's
hair and tells her that alone they
may be different leaves, but together,
they can always make a tree to enjoy the
sunshine or withstand the rain and wind.

"Brother, is a tree beautiful?" she asks.

"Yes, the beauty of working together goes
beyond the stars," he replies.

BEYOND THINKING: Together, anything is possible.

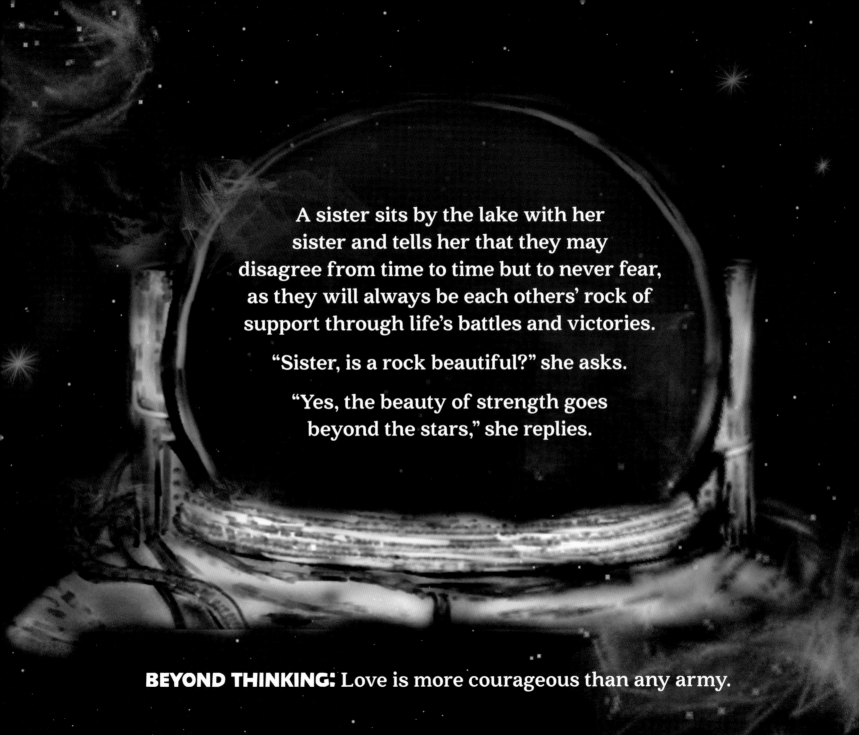

A sister sits by the lake with her
sister and tells her that they may
disagree from time to time but to never fear,
as they will always be each others' rock of
support through life's battles and victories.

"Sister, is a rock beautiful?" she asks.

"Yes, the beauty of strength goes
beyond the stars," she replies.

BEYOND THINKING: Love is more courageous than any army.

A father walks through the trails to
the mountain top with his daughter and
tells her about Earth, with all of its many
different countries, ethnicities, and nature and
the importance of keeping an open mind.

"Dad, are they all beautiful?" she asks.

"Yes, the beauty of the world and people
goes beyond the stars," he replies.

BEYOND THINKING: Don't divide, learn and explore.

An aunt plays in the field with her niece and tells her that while journeying through life there may be times she could be judged on her color or clothes but to never be discouraged, as these do not show her soul.

"Aunt, is a soul beautiful?" she asks.

"Yes, the beauty of accepting yourself goes beyond the stars," she replies.

BEYOND THINKING: The treasure of a soul.

An uncle walks through a tulip
field with his niece and tells her that
picking flowers by color is not hurtful but to
remember to be cautious, as this is not how she
should make friends throughout her lifetime.

"Uncle, are colors beautiful?" she asks.

"Yes, the beauty of expression goes
beyond the stars," he replies.

BEYOND THINKING: Colors cannot define people.

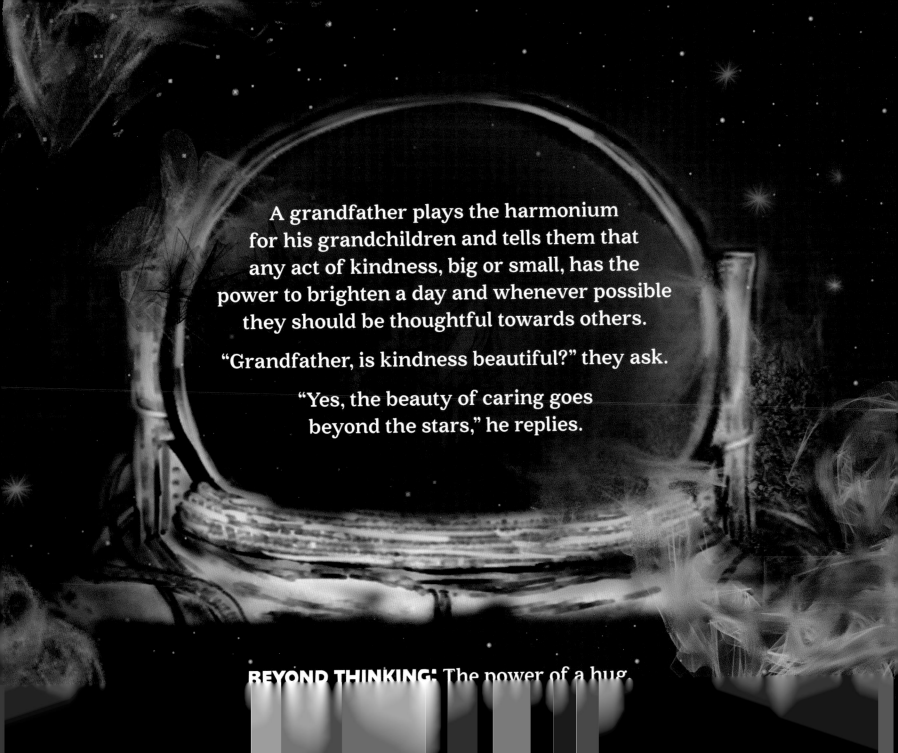

A grandfather plays the harmonium
for his grandchildren and tells them that
any act of kindness, big or small, has the
power to brighten a day and whenever possible
they should be thoughtful towards others.

"Grandfather, is kindness beautiful?" they ask.

"Yes, the beauty of caring goes
beyond the stars," he replies.

BEYOND THINKING: The power of a hug.

A grandmother walks with her grandchild through the woods and tells her that in life, every so often, her friends will be her teammates while her parents will be her coaches and to be mindful of her team.

"Grandmother, is a team beautiful?" she asks.

"Yes, the beauty of guidance and support goes beyond the stars," she replies.

BEYOND THINKING: A parent's advice is no enemy.

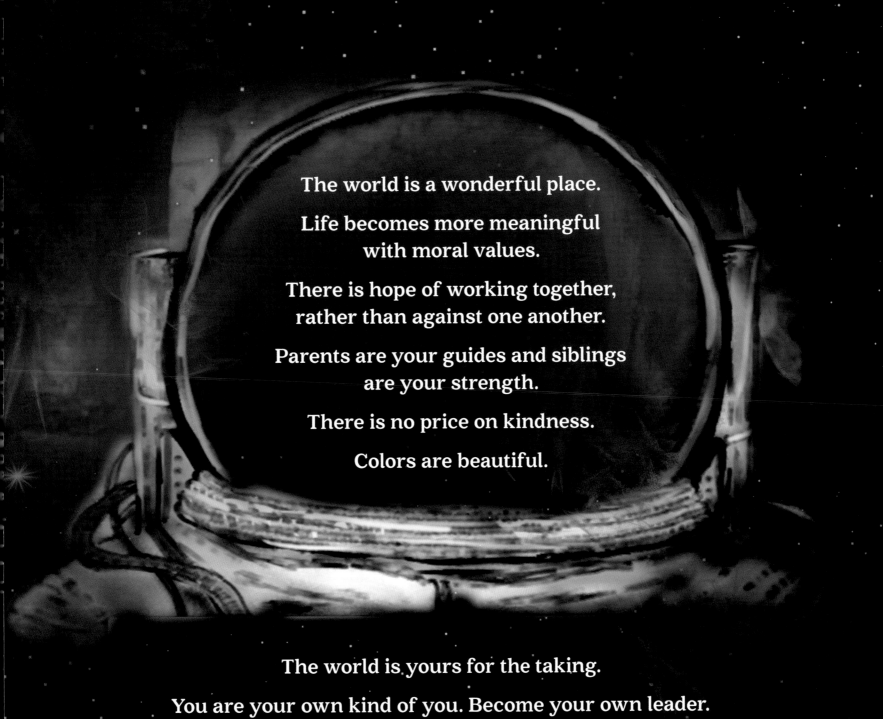

The world is a wonderful place.

Life becomes more meaningful
with moral values.

There is hope of working together,
rather than against one another.

Parents are your guides and siblings
are your strength.

There is no price on kindness.

Colors are beautiful.

The world is yours for the taking.

You are your own kind of you. Become your own leader.

THE END

ABOUT THE AUTHOR AND ILLUSTRATOR

TANYA KONDOLAY is of Indian origin and identifies herself as a Jat Sikh, Punjabi that was born and raised in Abbotsford, British Columbia in Canada. Her career is in the medical field; however, alongside finishing her medical degree, she decided to pursue her passion for the arts. Her affinity towards art was evident at a young age that began with drawing, progressed to painting, and transcended into dancing—traditional bhangra and ballet. She then went on to amalgamate her curiosity for expression further toward instruments by learning how to play the piano and guitar. Ultimately, she decided to embrace her love for words and drawing, extrapolating a newfound purpose, aside from medicine. With humility, she has transformed herself into both a writer and illustrator for childrens' literature as well.

A MOMENT OF GRATITUDE

Photographs were taken in various cities within Canada thoughtfully throughout the different seasons, in order to incorporate the natural beauty of Mother Nature. Ultimately, these photographs inspired my illustrations for this book.

In a world full of many choices—a heartfelt thank you to the photographer, photographed volunteers, and reader for making my vision come to life and selecting my book to read.

With Love,

Tanya Kondaleuy

ABOUT THE PHOTOGRAPHER

JULIE SIDORAK'S passion for photography was born many years ago from an always present love of art and design and authentic self-expression. Struggling with traditional learning as a child, art was always an outlet she could connect with and rely on. With this evolving and growing passion, she attended Nova Scotia College of Art and Design University, and in 2001, she completed her Bachelor of Fine Arts with a major in Photography, later joining Professional Photographers of Canada and Nikon Professional Services to further her education. This hunger for knowledge grew and eventually gave her the confidence she lacked as a child through the learning that just clicked. She loves to play with various mediums because of the freedom that it allows one to get. For she found that dancing to the beat of your own drum is a way to embrace one's differences and to realize that those very differences are beautiful and unique. She values authentic relationships; as such, connecting with people and discovering their truth, camera in hand, are magnificent moments for which she expresses much gratitude to experience.